Samuel French Acting Edition

What the Rabbi Saw

by Billy Van Zandt
and Jane Milmore

I0591766

ǁ **SAMUEL FRENCH** ǁ

SAMUELFRENCH.COM   SAMUELFRENCH.CO.UK

FOR PRODUCTION ENQUIRIES

UNITED STATES AND CANADA
Info@SamuelFrench.com
1-866-598-8449

UNITED KINGDOM AND EUROPE
Plays@SamuelFrench.co.uk
020-7255-4302

Each title is subject to availability from Samuel French, depending upon country of performance. Please be aware that *WHAT THE RABBI SAW* may not be licensed by Samuel French in your territory. Professional and amateur producers should contact the nearest Samuel French office or licensing partner to verify availability.

MUSIC USE NOTE

Licensees are solely responsible for obtaining formal written permission from copyright owners to use copyrighted music in the performance of this play and are strongly cautioned to do so. If no such permission is obtained by the licensee, then the licensee must use only original music that the licensee owns and controls. Licensees are solely responsible and liable for all music clearances and shall indemnify the copyright owners of the play(s) and their licensing agent, Samuel French, against any costs, expenses, losses and liabilities arising from the use of music by licensees. Please contact the appropriate music licensing authority in your territory for the rights to any incidental music.

IMPORTANT BILLING AND CREDIT REQUIREMENTS

If you have obtained performance rights to this title, please refer to your licensing agreement for important billing and credit requirements.

WHAT THE RABBI SAW was first produced by Mark Fleming at the Henderson Theater in Lincroft, New Jersey on May 18, 1995. The performance was directed by Billy Van Zandt and Art Neill, with sets by Mark Fleming, costumes by Kitty Cleary, and lighting and sound by B.J. Smith. The Production Stage Managers were Neil Murphy and Sue Kulinyi. The cast was as follows:

WALTER	Billy Van Zandt
CLAUDIA	Sally Void Winters
MRS. KIRSCHENBAUM	Sherle Tallent
RABBI HUCHELMAN	Drew Hollywood
WENDY	Jane Milmore
MITCH	Glenn Jones
NOEL	Michael Kroll
MR. KIRSCHENBAUM	Tom Frascatore
LAINIE BERMAN	Adrienne Barbeau
VINNIE	Art Neill
EDDIE	Ian Gonzalez

CHARACTERS

WALTER – The Groom
WENDY – The Bride
CLAUDIA – The Bridesmaid
MITCH – The Best Man
LAINIE BERMAN – The Singer
NOEL – The Wedding Coordinator
MR. KIRSCHENBAUM – The Father of the Bride
MRS. KIRSCHENBAUM – The Mother of the Bride
RABBI HUCHELMAN – The Rabbi
VINNIE – The Uninvited Guest
EDDIE – The Wedding Photographer

SETTING

Waldorf Astoria Hotel, New York City

TIME

1995

ACT I

(Curtain rises on a hotel suite in the Waldorf Astoria Hotel, NYC. It is furnished elegantly in a traditional style. A large king-size bed sits center stage against the back wall. Night tables are on either side of the bed. A door to the hotel hallway is down-stage right. Up-stage of the door are a writing table and chair, where a phone sits. Up-stage of the desk, at an angle are two sliding closet doors. Up-stage left of the bed is an open hallway with a sink that leads off to the bathroom up-stage center (behind the headboard). Stage left of the bathroom arch are two french doors leading out to a balcony that over-looks Central Park and a New York skyline. Down-stage left is a low armoire that houses a TV and a bar set-up. Down-stage left is the door to an adjoining room.)

(As the action begins, we see a TUXEDOED MAN and a MAID OF HONOR frolicking on the bed. THEY are WALTER and CLAUDIA. THEY are dressed but quite disheveled)

WALTER: Claudia ... please. Please. We have to get downstairs.

CLAUDIA: Not yet.

WALTER: Claudia, please. The wedding's gonna start any time now.

CLAUDIA: The wedding's not until nine-fifteen. We

7

have plenty of time.

WALTER: But ... Claudia, the guests are arriving ... people are waiting ...

CLAUDIA: Let 'em wait.

WALTER: They'll be wondering.

CLAUDIA: Let them wonder.

WALTER: But ... but our parents are here and ... !

CLAUDIA: Walter, my mother's waited her whole life for this wedding. She can wait another hour.

WALTER: You're an animal, Claudia.

CLAUDIA: I don't care, Walter. I'll never see you again after today.

WALTER: How can you say that? I'm marrying your sister. I'll see you all the time.

CLAUDIA: Yes, but it can never be the same between us, after you and Wendy say "I do." That's a line I just won't cross.

(There's a knock at the door.)

FEMALE VOICE: *(off)* Walter Saltzman? Are you in there? You open this door right this minute.

CLAUDIA: It's my mother.

WALTER: I told you we should have gone downstairs!

CLAUDIA: What do we do?

WALTER: Uh ... Don't panic. Just don't panic. *(calling)* I'll be right there, Mrs. Kirschenbaum! *(to CLAUDIA)* Get dressed and go out through the adjoining room. Quick!

CLAUDIA: It's locked from the other side!

WALTER: *(buttoning his shirt up)* Oh. Then just get dressed. I'll handle her.

CLAUDIA: I can't.

WALTER: What do you mean you can't?

CLAUDIA: We're stuck!

WALTER: What do you mean we're stuck? Stuck how?

CLAUDIA: Stuck-stuck.

WALTER: You mean, like dogs-stuck?

CLAUDIA: No! Stuck like your-zipper-is-caught-in-my-taffeta-stuck.

WALTER: Are you kidding?

CLAUDIA: Hey, watch it. Don't rip my dress. Wendy will kill me!

WALTER: Okay. Listen to me. Forget the old plan. Here's the new plan: Panic!

MRS. KIRSCHENBAUM: *(off) (pounding on the door)* Open this door, Mr. Saltzman!

WALTER: I'm dead. I'm dead. I'm a dead man.

CLAUDIA: Oh, and I suppose I'm not a dead man?

WALTER: I got it. Get on top of me and say "come in."

CLAUDIA: I'm not playing that again, Walter. My mother's at the door.

WALTER: Are you an idiot, Claudia? Just do it.

MRS. KIRSCHENBAUM: *(off)* What are you doing in there, Walter! Open up. I have a key and I'm coming in! I know you're in there! It's Mrs. Kirschenbaum!

WALTER: Hurry up.

(WALTER lays down, CLAUDIA sits on the bed. WALTER drapes the bedspread over his torso, leaving his legs dangling off the bed like they're coming out of CLAUDIA's skirt. WALTER's pant legs are hiked up, revealing black socks, garters, and hairy legs. MRS. KIRSCHENBAUM enters.)

MRS. KIRSCHENBAUM: Claudia! Where the hell is Walter? Rabbi Huchelman needs him to sign the Katuba.

CLAUDIA: Where is *Walter?* Oh, he ... uh ... he ... *(WALTER's arm pops out through CLAUDIA's arm hole and points off)* He ... left. *(WALTER waves good-bye) (calling off)* Bye-bye. Bye-bye. There he goes. Bye, Walter. *(WALTER mumbles "Bye-Bye")* You must have just passed him in the hall.

MRS. KIRSCHENBAUM: Oh. Well, get up. You should be next door helping your sister dress. What kind of maid of honor are you?

CLAUDIA: I had to get dressed all by *my*self, Mother.

(WALTER adjusts a stocking or bra strap.)

MRS. KIRSCHENBAUM: Your sister's getting married in one hour. One hour! I have a lot on my mind. And the last thing I need is an argument from you. *(WALTER mimes that she's a blabbermouth)* Don't you make fun of me, young lady! *(she slaps WALTER's hand, he makes a fist back at her) (gasps)* Good God, Claudia, look at your legs. *(WALTER feels her legs)* And after all your father and I spent on electrolysis.

CLAUDIA: I know, Mom.

MRS. KIRSCHENBAUM: Did it grow back on your shoulders, too?

CLAUDIA: No, Mom.

(CLAUDIA slaps WALTER's hand as it feels for her back.)

MRS. KIRSCHENBAUM: Well, my God, Claudia! We have over 200 guests coming. Doctors, lawyers and seven accountants. All single. The least you can do is shave your legs. Who knows when I'll get you another opportunity like this? *(MRS. KIRSCHENBAUM leans over to get a shaving kit off the desk. WALTER thumbs CLAUDIA's nose)* Now. You've got exactly one hour to look presentable. Here. Use your father's razor and shave those hedges.

CLAUDIA: But Mom. Hairy legs are the latest rage.

MRS. KIRSCHENBAUM: No. *(indicates herself)* Here's your latest rage. *(she hands CLAUDIA an electric razor)* Look, Claudia Rachel Kirschenbaum, you know your sister's throwing you the bouquet! And I'll be damned if I'll let all those single men watch them put a garter on my monkey-legged daughter. Here.

WALTER: *(off-stage)* No!

MRS. KIRSCHENBAUM: Did you say "no" to me?

CLAUDIA: No.

MRS. KIRSCHENBAUM: It sure sounded like "no."

CLAUDIA: Mom, you know you're having trouble with your hearing. Fun-gee-pa-nan.

MRS. KIRSCHENBAUM: What?

CLAUDIA: See?

MRS. KIRSCHENBAUM: Knock it off. Now shave those legs!

CLAUDIA: Well, okay. Well, here goes nothing ...

(CLAUDIA shaves WALTER's legs. WALTER's screams come from CLAUDIA's accommodatingly open mouth. WALTER keeps kicking his legs. MRS. KIRSCHENBAUM's eyes bug out as she watches.)

WALTER: *(off-stage)* Oooowwww ... oh-oh-oh-oh-ow,

you're killing me ... stop it. Oh-oh-oh ... Mm!!!
MRS. KIRSCHENBAUM: What did you say?
CLAUDIA: Nothing. I just said ...

(She shaves his legs again. He screams all over again.)

WALTER: *(off-stage)* Oooowwww ... oh-oh-oh-oh-ow,
you're killing me ... stop it. Oh-oh-oh ... Mm!!!
MRS. KIRSCHENBAUM: Well, what is that supposed
to mean?

(WALTER pulls CLAUDIA's hair.)

CLAUDIA: Ow!
MRS. KIRSCHENBAUM: What is the matter with you?
CLAUDIA: I keep nicking myself. Take that!

(She shaves more. WALTER struggles and screams.)

WALTER: *(off-stage)* Oooowww ... oh-oh-oh-oh-oh-oh-
oh-oh ... Mm!!!

(WALTER stuffs his fingers up her nose.)

CLAUDIA: Ow! Ow!
MRS. KIRSCHENBAUM: What the hell is the matter
with you? Stop that, Claudia. Get your fingers out of your
nose! You did that in the car all the way up here. Don't think
your father and I weren't watching you. *(CLAUDIA slaps the
hand twice. And the third time, WALTER removes his hand
and she slaps herself in the face by mistake)* What are you

doing? Have you lost your mind? *(WALTER grabs her breast and squeezes. CLAUDIA writhes in agony)* For Christ's Sake! Claudia! What on earth is the matter with you? They're big enough. Stop touching them. What are you doing to yourself? *(CLAUDIA sits hard. WALTER's castrated legs cross themselves in pain)* What in hell is wrong with you? Has that rash come back?

CLAUDIA: No, Mom.

MRS. KIRSCHENBAUM: Get up, young lady. Right now!

CLAUDIA: I can't, Mom.

MRS. KIRSCHENBAUM: You can't what?

CLAUDIA: I can't ... let you go downstairs looking like that.

MRS. KIRSCHENBAUM: Looking like what?

CLAUDIA: Your make-up is all smeared.

(WALTER's hand wipes across MRS. KIRSCHENBAUM's face. Her lipstick smears. She looks in the mirror.)

MRS. KIRSCHENBAUM: It is? Omigod. I look like your Aunt Fran when she eats pizza. Where's the bathroom?

(WALTER motions "that way." MRS. KIRSCHENBAUM exits into the bathroom. WALTER and CLAUDIA climb off the bed.)

CLAUDIA: *(calling)* Take your time, Mom!
WALTER: You shaved my leg!
CLAUDIA: You picked my nose!
WALTER: You had hair on your back?

CLAUDIA: Quick. Take your pants off. I can go borrow tux pants from a waiter and come back for you.

(WALTER takes his pants off. RABBI HUCHELMAN enters just as WALTER is undressed. The RABBI sees CLAUDIA and a pantless WALTER holding WALTER's pants in the air.)

RABBI: Walter?

WALTER: Rabbi Huchelman?

RABBI: Did I come at a bad time?

WALTER: No. What makes you say that?

RABBI: I'm here for the signing of the Katuba. What's with the "no pants?" Is everything all right?

WALTER: Yes. In fact, we were just coming to get you.

CLAUDIA: We were? I mean, we were. We were.

RABBI: Then it's a good thing I wasn't there. *(he laughs at his own joke)* So what did you need me for that couldn't wait?

WALTER: Well, you see, Rabbi, everyone knows there's a prayer for the wine and a prayer for the bread, but we have an old family wedding custom where we pray over the pants.

RABBI: Over the pants?

WALTER: Sort of a "go forth and multiply" sort of thing.

RABBI: I never heard of such a thing.

WALTER: Well, it happens.

RABBI: I'm used to the Orthodox.

WALTER: Who isn't?

RABBI: You want me to ...

WALTER: If you don't mind.

RABBI: Not at all.

(He goes to take the pants. CLAUDIA backs away, clutching the pants.)

CLAUDIA: It's also part of the custom that the maid of honor holds the pants while you pray.

RABBI: I didn't know that. *(as he prays, MRS. KIRSCHENBAUM enters and sees the scene) (praying)* May your seed be plentiful. May your offspring follow in the path of the righteous. And may your pants break just right over the tops of your shoes.

MRS. KIRSCHENBAUM: What the hell are you doing?

(WALTER motions that the RABBI is drunk.)

RABBI: We're praying over the pants.

MRS. KIRSCHENBAUM: I told you to stay out of the Manischevitz, Rabbi Huchelman.

RABBI: It's an old wedding custom.

MRS. KIRSCHENBAUM: Here's a new wedding custom, Huchelman. It's called get downstairs and eat something to soak up that alcohol.

RABBI: You know, I was eyeing those stuffed mushrooms. They looked tasty.

MRS. KIRSCHENBAUM: Fine. Eat some stuffed mushrooms and sober up. Just stay away from the rum balls, got it? *(she shoves HUCHELMAN out the door)* And you two better be ready when I come out of the bathroom! Look at me. I've eaten so many cheese balls, I look like I'm pregnant.

WALTER: *(muttered)* Yeah, blame it on the cheeseballs.

(MRS. KIRSCHENBAUM exits to the bathroom. From the adjoining room we hear:)

WENDY: *(off-stage)* Walter? Are you in there? *(from the adjoining room, WENDY, the distraught bride, sweeps in. WALTER runs for the bathroom, realizes he can't hide in there, then hits the floor. WENDY wears her wedding gown with its large train. In a panic, CLAUDIA grabs WENDY's hands and turns her back to WALTER, who crawls around trying to find a place to hide) (crying)* Oh, Claudia. I don't know what to do. We have a room full of people and Mommy and Daddy spent all this money and everything is such a mess.

CLAUDIA: Wendy, stay down ... calm down.

WENDY: Calm down? Walter's missing! No one can find him. What am I going to do? I have to find him. We have all these guests. And Lainie Berman is flying in all the way from Las Vegas just to sing when I walk down the aisle. Where could he have gone?

(WALTER panics and crawls under the drapes. He bulges out ridiculously too much. CLAUDIA sees this and panics.)

CLAUDIA: Don't worry. Walter's not going to stand you up. How could he when you look so beautiful? He's gonna take one look at you in this dress and go nuts.

(She steers WENDY to WALTER and hides WALTER under WENDY's train. As WENDY walks around the room, he will follow her, unseen by WENDY.)

WENDY: Well ... where *is* he?

CLAUDIA: He's probably taking care of last minute things. You know how Walter is. He's got his nose into everything.

WENDY: *(walking stage right. Her "train" follows)* You don't suppose he changed his mind, do you?

CLAUDIA: Of course not.

WENDY: I'm going to be a laughing stock. The family laughing stock. *(she walks stage left, leaving WALTER behind who is unaware she's moved. Still with his eyes covered)* But hey, why should today be any different? I screwed up my entire life so what else is new?

(CLAUDIA sees WALTER at the foot of the bed – his eyes covered. He is unaware he is in plain sight. CLAUDIA steers WENDY back to WALTER and drapes WENDY's train over his head.)

CLAUDIA: Wendy, stop crying. Here. Have a drink. That'll calm you down.

WENDY: You know I don't drink.

CLAUDIA: Just one. Come on. It will relax you. It'll make you a radiant bride.

WENDY: *(sucking down a drink)* Okay. But just one.

CLAUDIA: And don't worry about Walter. He's probably right under your feet somewhere. You look like a fairy princess. He's not standing you up.

WENDY: "Standing me up?" I'm not worried he's standing me up.

CLAUDIA: Then what's wrong?

WENDY: I don't know how to say this, Claudia. But I

can't keep it in any longer. We went to all this trouble and now everything is all screwed up. *(she hands back empty glass. She walks left again. The "train" follows)* Daddy is going to kill me.

CLAUDIA: What are you trying to say?

WENDY: There's someone else.

CLAUDIA: What do you mean?

WENDY: What do you think I mean?

CLAUDIA: Walter's having an affair?

WENDY: Worse. *(she removes her bouquet and veil drape to reveal a rolled up pair of men's tuxedo pants attached to her gown)* I am!

(WENDY walks right. WALTER again is left behind. And so is a man in a tuxedo. This is MITCH.)

MITCH: *(after a very long beat)* Is it hot in here or is it just me?

WENDY: Omigod.

CLAUDIA: Omi*god!*

WALTER: I was wondering what was grabbing my arm under there.

WENDY: What were you doing back there?

WALTER: Never mind me. What was my best friend doing back there?

CLAUDIA: Yeah, Mitch. What *were* you doing back there?

MITCH: Uh ... Looking for the ring? *(fakes pulling ring out of dress)* There it is!

WENDY: What were you and Claudia doing in here with no pants on?

WALTER: Oh, we were ... we were ... well, not at first we weren't ... Don't change the subject.

WENDY: You're having an affair!

WALTER: We are not. There's a perfectly reasonable explanation for why I don't have any pants on.

WENDY: Like what?

WALTER: Claudia? Tell her.

CLAUDIA: We're having an affair.

WALTER: There. See? We're having an affair ... no!

WENDY: Omigod. I need another drink.

WALTER: A drink? You drink now, too? Who *are* you?! Who *is* this person?

WENDY: *(crying)* I don't know!

WALTER: How could you do this to me?

CLAUDIA: Who cares? They're having an affair! You heard her, Walter.

WALTER: I couldn't hear anything under there. Between her thighs and his wheezing it was like the Cone of Silence down there.

WENDY: Well, now what are we going to do?

CLAUDIA: There's only one thing to do.

WALTER, WENDY & MITCH: What?

CLAUDIA: You've got to call off the wedding.

WALTER & WENDY: We can't call off the wedding.

WALTER: We invited guests.

WENDY: The musicians are already here.

WALTER: They're already passing the hors d'oeuvres, for Christ's Sake.

WENDY: And in case you haven't noticed, I'm in my dress already!

CLAUDIA: Well, you can't go through with this now.

You don't even love each other.

WALTER: Did she mention the musicians are already here?

CLAUDIA: I know. You can marry *me*, Walter.

WENDY: Yeah. Right. Like you could ever fit into this dress.

CLAUDIA: Come on, Walter. It'll be perfect. The guest list wouldn't even have to change very much.

WENDY: This is my wedding, Claudia. And if anybody's getting married, it's gonna be me!

MITCH: This is insane.

CLAUDIA: You always have to be the center of attention, don't you?

WENDY: *(taking another hit of vodka)* Yes, I do.

CLAUDIA: Fine. Then just marry Mitch.

MITCH: *(doing spit take with drink)* Now, wait a minute here ...

WALTER: "Mitch?" My parents didn't come here to watch anybody marry Mitch.

MITCH: I am not gonna stand here and be insulted. Let's go, Wendy.

WALTER: Oh. You're not going anywhere. In fact, the only place you're going ... is to hell!

(WALTER charges at MITCH and chokes him. WALTER and MITCH pummel each other behind the women's backs.)

CLAUDIA: How could you cheat on a man like Walter? Everything he's ever done, he's done for you.

WENDY: He slept with you behind my back!

CLAUDIA: Well, except for that.

WENDY: Somebody's coming! *(the door opens and NOEL the wedding planner enters. He carries a fruit basket and a floral arrangement. The men freeze their strangulation pose and segue into two pals with their arms around each other. The girls cover their attached pants with a bouquet and a room service menu.)* It's Noel, my wedding coordinator!

NOEL: Here comes the bride ... all dressed in ... *(taking in room)* Jesus, Mary and sweet St. Sondheim. Wendy, Walter, Mitchell, Claudia. What are you all doing in this room? This is Lainie Berman's room. I specifically assigned you the room next door and ... Wendy, what are you doing?!

WENDY: I don't know.

NOEL: You are not supposed to wear your train until "magic time." You want to look like you're dragging a dirty old Kleenex back here? *(he unhooks the train)* Look, threads already. All this money and you're going to look like a Rastafarian.

(NOEL cuts a thread off her train and puts the scissors on the desk where he also lays the train.)

WALTER: Nobody's going to be looking at her. They're going to be too busy gawking at me in my underwear!

NOEL: Don't be too sure. I ... Where are your pants?

WALTER: You tell us, Mr. Wedding Planner.

MITCH: You never gave us any.

NOEL: What do you mean?

WALTER: What do you think we mean? Look at us. Tux jacket, cummerbund, boutonniere ...

MITCH: Shirt, socks, bow tie ... but ...

WENDY & CLAUDIA: No pants.

NOEL: No pants? How did I not notice this?

WALTER: Mr. Kirschenbaum is going to have a fit when he sees what a slip-shod job you've done with this wedding.

NOEL: Slip-shod? Slip-shod?! I have live swans in a man-made lake in the middle of the ballroom. Baby roses hand-dyed to match the lobster appetizer. And an ice sculpture of the house Wendy was born in! Don't tell me I'm doing a slip-shod job you arrogant little piece of shit.

MITCH: Nice mouth.

WENDY: They still have no pants, Noel!

WALTER: Yeah. We were hoping they were delivered to this room by mistake, but no such luck.

NOEL: But I personally went through each and every rental ...

WALTER: Well, not good enough, apparently.

CLAUDIA: Daddy's paying you good money to coordinate this wedding, Noel. So try coordinating some pants or should we just call Daddy now and let you answer to him?

NOEL: No! For God's Sake no! Don't tell your father about the pants. Don't panic. Nobody panic. I'm sure I can find two pair of tuxedo pants in an hour's notice in Manhattan on a holiday weekend. Leave it to me. I'll get them. And don't worry. When I get through with you, you'll look like a prince! A prince, I tell you! *(handing fruit basket to WALTER)* Here, prince.

(He exits.)

MITCH: Quick thinking, Walter.

WALTER: Thank you, Mitch.

MITCH: You always were quick on your feet.

WALTER: Yeah. And you've always been right there with me. Sharing my ups, my downs. My highs, my lows.

CLAUDIA: My sister, your fiancee ...

WALTER: It's a shame I have to kill you now.

(He starts throwing oranges from a fruit basket at MITCH, who retreats behind the bar.)

MITCH: Cut it out. You know what citric acid can do to a person's eyes?

WALTER: Not enough. Quick. Claudia, find me some bricks. Mess around with my wife ...

MITCH: You're a lunatic. A crazy freaking lunatic!

CLAUDIA: Good Mitch. Piss him off.

(Oranges fly by. MITCH holds up a room service menu as a shield, batting them away.)

WENDY: I'm not even your wife for another hour, Walter.

(She swigs from the bottle now.)

MITCH: Yeah. Technically she's still up for grabs. I mean ... well, not grabs, maybe ... *(lowering menu)* $10.99 for a hamburger? *(an orange hits him in the head)* Oh, that's gonna bruise.

MRS. KIRSCHENBAUM: *(off)* What's going on out there?

(SFX: Toilet flush.)

(All freeze.)

CLAUDIA: My mother's coming! Omigod.
MITCH: Pants!

(They all look down at their pantless condition. WALTER quickly jumps into the pants attached to WENDY, MITCH to the ones attached to CLAUDIA. MRS. KIRSCHENBAUM enters drying her hands with a towel.)

MRS. KIRSCHENBAUM: What is going on out here, Wendy Rebeccah Kirschenbaum? What are you doing in this room! Don't you know it's bad luck to see the groom before the wedding?
WENDY: It is?
MITCH: *(rubbing his head)* It was for me.
MRS. KIRSCHENBAUM: Get moving, ladies. Out of sight. *(she starts to push WENDY and CLAUDIA. The boys follow)* And where do you boys think you're going?
WALTER: No where.
MRS. KIRSCHENBAUM: Then go over there.
WALTER: Okay.

(They do and the girls follow.)

MRS. KIRSCHENBAUM: Wendy, Claudia. You come with me.
CLAUDIA: Okay, Mom.

(They do and the boys follow.)

MRS. KIRSCHENBAUM: Can't anyone hear me? Where are you going?

WALTER: Oh, we're ... we're just practicing walking down the aisle.

WENDY: Yeah, Mom. After all you and Daddy put into this wedding you wouldn't want us to screw it up, would you?

MRS. KIRSCHENBAUM: Well, no, but ...

MITCH: Is it left right left right or left left right right?

CLAUDIA: See?

(The door opens and MR. KIRSCHENBAUM enters. He is an asshole blowhard with a bad toupee.)

MR. KIRSCHENBAUM: Lainie, I ... what's going on here? Wendy? Claudia?

WENDY & CLAUDIA: Hi, Daddy.

(WENDY hiccups.)

MR. KIRSCHENBAUM: What on God's green earth do you think you're doing? Your room is next door. This is Lainie Berman's room.

MRS. KIRSCHENBAUM: Hello, dear.

MR. KIRSCHENBAUM: Don't "hello dear" me. I rented two rooms. One for all of us to change our clothes in, and one for Lainie Berman. This is not the one for you. Get out. Look at this place. What are you people, animals?

MRS. KIRSCHENBAUM: Is everything all right, Harry?

(She starts to clean up the ice and dry the floor with a towel.)

MR. KIRSCHENBAUM: Nobody'll ever accuse you of being a genius, will they, Edie? Of course everything is not all right. Your cousins brought their uninvited kids, the air conditioning is on the blink, and I have no Lainie Berman! You know how much money I had to spend to fly her in from Vegas to sing at this wedding?

ALL: Plenty.

MR. KIRSCHENBAUM: Plenty. I had to pay through the wahoo for a big star like her. But where is she? Who knows! And what do you think is gonna happen when she doesn't show up? Chaos, that's what. Chaos. Who's going to sing when Wendy here walks down the aisle? You?

MRS. KIRSCHENBAUM: If I have to I will.

MR. KIRSCHENBAUM: Don't even entertain that thought. Have you ever heard yourself sing? *(as his wife, singing)* "Hee Haw. Hee Haw."

WALTER: I don't even know who Lainie Berman is.

MR. KIRSCHENBAUM: Then you're an idiot. She's a big star. A big star. And it wasn't easy getting her to sing at your wedding either, bright-light. So get out of this room. She's a star and she better feel special. Got it?

WENDY: Lainie Berman. Lainie Berman. This is *my* wedding, daddy.

MR. KIRSCHENBAUM: What did you say? You're not too big to put over my knee, you know.

WENDY: Nothing.

CLAUDIA: Daddy, she's just saying ...

MR. KIRSCHENBAUM: What are you, her translator? You're not too big to put over my knee either.

MRS. KIRSCHENBAUM: Dear, she's just saying ...

MR. KIRSCHENBAUM: And you ... *(waves away the*

rest of the thought) Now, clean this room up. You want Lainie
Berman to think we're your mother's family?

(They try moving together in pairs.)

MRS. KIRSCHENBAUM: *(picking up fruit and fixing
the bed)* Your father's right.

MR. KIRSCHENBAUM: Of course I'm right. I'm
always right. I've only been wrong *once. (he looks at his wife
to emphasize the point)* Make that bed up and clean up the
floor. Now, Wendy.

WENDY: But Daddy, I'm already dressed for my
wedding.

MR. KIRSCHENBAUM: And you know how much
frigging upholstered furniture I had to sell to buy that dress?

ALL: Plenty.

MR. KIRSCHENBAUM: Plenty, let me tell you. Jesus,
Edie, what kind of daughters did you raise for me? I'm out
breaking my hump to pay for the capped teeth, and the
electrolysis, and sanding down those big gaping facial pores
they inherited from your side of the family and for what? For
this? No goddam respect. No goddam respect at all, I tell you!

WALTER: I respect you, sir.

MR. KIRSCHENBAUM: Shut up, kiss ass. Did you sign
the pre-nup?

WALTER: Yes.

MR. KIRSCHENBAUM: Good. Get away from me.
Come on, Edie! We have guests.

MRS. KIRSCHENBAUM: Coming, Harry.

MR. KIRSCHENBAUM: Let's go. Chop-chop. Let's go,
Edie. Don't just stand there with your mouth hanging open.

(They exit.)

MITCH: Ooh. And they say Hitler didn't *have* any children.

WALTER: *(laughs, then:)* Hey, that's my future father-in-law you're talking about. You think I forgot what's going on here?

MITCH: I was hoping.

(Everyone begins to get teary during the following:)

WALTER: My fiancee and my best friend. God was I stupid not to see this. How could you? How could you! After all we've been through ... Mitch.

WENDY: "Mitch?" What the hell am I?

WALTER: Huh? Oh. You're right, Wendy. I owe you an explanation. I'm in love with your sister. There. I said it. *(taking CLAUDIA's hand)* I'm in love with Claudia. I have been from the second she had her nose fixed.

WENDY: Two months ago?

CLAUDIA: *(taking her hand back to gesture)* Yes. Two months ago last Tuesday.

(WALTER takes MITCH's hand thinking it's CLAUDIA's, kisses it.)

WENDY: How did this happen?

CLAUDIA: Well, remember those two weeks you and Walter weren't speaking?

WENDY: *(tucking her head under WALTER's arm)* The week the invitations went out?

CLAUDIA: Yes. Anyway, you were out having your bridal fitting, and, well, I was on my way home from having a free makeover at Bloomingdale's, because the swelling had gone down and I had a coupon. And as I walked out of Bloomie's onto Lexington, who do I see but Walter.

WALTER: It was a great nose job. We were in bed two hours before I realized who she was. And by then ... I didn't care.

(They all sit on the bed, tangled together.)

WENDY: Oh, God. This is such a complete mess.

(WALTER tries crossing his leg over MITCH's, it can't get there. Finally he heaves it up and over, castrating himself silently.)

WALTER: What about you two?

WENDY: Remember last New Year's Eve when you had that fight with Daddy and he shoved you out the front door?

WALTER: Yeah.

MITCH: And remember how you slipped on that icy patch and cracked your head on that statue of the little jockey?

WALTER: Yeah.

WENDY: And remember how you were in a coma for eight days and nobody knew whether you were going to live or die?

WALTER: Yeah.

MITCH: Well, I kept coming to the hospital and Wendy was always there, and, well, one thing led to another ... and ...

there *was* that extra bed in the room ...

WALTER: *(rising)* Wait a minute. This started when I was laying there dying in the hospital?

MITCH: Yeah.

WALTER: *Five* months ago? While I was laying there with tubes up my nose?

MITCH: Jesus, Walter. We thought you were gonna die.

WALTER: I'll kill you, you son of a bitch!

(WALTER tries to kill MITCH again – which is difficult since they are all stuck together between pants, and hand holding and twisted arms. MITCH runs away, dragging the others who are still attached. WALTER knees MITCH in the butt as they hop around.)

MITCH: Not again. *(to CLAUDIA)* Come on, you big moose. Move it.

CLAUDIA: Who are you calling a moose?

(CLAUDIA slaps MITCH in the hand. WENDY hangs on WALTER's hands. Eventually they all tip over and fall to the floor. WALTER still tries to strangle MITCH. The foursome rolls back and forth across the stage, locked together in a strangulation dance. They roll across the room to the left, all the way back to stage right, and back again to stage left, finally resting all their weight on MITCH, who screams for air.)

WALTER: Ow. Who's keys are those?

MITCH: Get off me. You're crushing my lungs.

WALTER: Move. Claudia, get your fat ass off me. I can't breathe.

MITCH: Good.

(They all lie face up on the floor, panting.)

CLAUDIA: "Fat ass?"

(CLAUDIA slugs WALTER.)

WALTER: Ow.

(They all lay flat on the floor, exhausted. NOEL re-enters with two pair of tuxedo pants on a single hanger.)

NOEL: Here, I found your pants. Don't ask questions and ... don't go anywhere near the kitchen. I ... What are you doing now?

(They all do sit-ups in unison.)

ALL: 98, 99, 100!
WALTER: Now let's do jumping jacks.
NOEL: *(dropping pants and pulling WALTER and CLAUDIA up)* Get up. Are you crazy? You're wrinkling the tuxes! These are rentals, people! *(pulling up MITCH and CLAUDIA)* You heard your father, Wendy. You can't be in this room. This is reserved for ... where did you get those pants?
WALTER: Uh ... these pants?
NOEL: Yes.
WALTER: The ones I'm wearing?

(CLAUDIA notices the doubles in tux pants now, so she takes the two new pair NOEL just brought in and hangs them off the back of NOEL's jacket.)

NOEL: Yes!

WALTER: You just gave them to us.

NOEL: *(turning around)* I did?

WENDY: Yes.

MITCH: Five minutes ago.

NOEL: *(turning back and forth)* I did not. I just ... put them ... over ... Where did I put them?

WALTER: You just gave them to us.

NOEL: Are you sure?

WALTER: Would we make something like that up?

WENDY: You just handed them to Walter and Mitch.

NOEL: I did? Oh, the stress is killing me. They sent white roses instead of the pink. They folded the napkins like tee-pees instead of peacock tails. The place cards don't say "Wendy and Walter." They say "Wandy and Welter." Like Welter's even a name. And now this? Oh. Well. Not your problem. Let's see. Show me the pants. *(the men model. WALTER's are too short, MITCH's too long)* Welcome back from the dead, Laurel and Hardy. You're wearing each other's pants. *(the men look down) (to WALTER)* Your pants are too short. *(to MITCH)* And yours are too long.

WALTER: Oh, yeah. We noticed that. But we thought this is how you wanted us to wear them.

(WALTER and MITCH model their ill-fitting pants.)

NOEL: Did it ever occur to you to try switching?

CLAUDIA: How do you think we got into this mess in the first place?

(Telephone.)

NOEL: Don't panic. I'll get it. Switch pants, both of you. Right now. *(as NOEL answers the phone, the boys get out of their tux pants) (into phone)* Hello – hello, Noel the wedding coordinator speaking. Yes? You don't say. You don't say.

(Hangs up.)

WENDY: Who was it?
NOEL: He didn't say. But ... Miss Berman has arrived. Don't panic. I can't feel my legs. It's okay. I'm fine. Miss Berman is here. She's coming up. Get out.
WENDY: You go ahead. We'll straighten the room up.
NOEL: Promise?
CLAUDIA: Promise. Don't worry about us. We'll be changed and gone before you get back.

(WALTER points to NOEL's back, where the two pair of pants hang off and motions "Get Them.")

NOEL: You better be. If not I'll be johnny in the hot seat. *(NOEL turns to leave. MITCH tries grabbing the extra pair of pants off NOEL's jacket)* What are you doing?
MITCH: Nothing.

(MITCH frozen in a strange position segues into a flamenco dance. NOEL backs out.)

WENDY: Good one, Claudia. He just walked out with the pants.

WALTER: We lost the pants.

MITCH: We're screwed.

WALTER: How hard can it be to get two pair of pants?

CLAUDIA: Pretty hard, so far.

(There is a knock at the door.)

RABBI: *(off)* Walter, are you in there?

WALTER: Rabbi Huchelman!

RABBI: *(off)* We still didn't sign the Katuba.

WENDY: Pants. Fast!

(The foursome panic. The men try leaping into the pants but keep missing and falling. RABBI HUCHELMAN enters to witness this.)

RABBI: What's with the leaping and the prancing?

WENDY & CLAUDIA: Rabbi Huchelman.

RABBI: What is this? Another custom?

WALTER: What are you talking about?

RABBI: You're leaping in your underpants. What am I, seeing things?

WALTER: Yes, yes, I guess you are seeing things. Because ... we're ... not leaping. And ... we ... we definitely aren't in our underpants.

MITCH: *(sotto)* Then whose underpants are these?

WALTER: *(sotto)* Shut up. *(to RABBI)* As you can see, Rabbi Huchelman, Mitch and I are clearly not leaping and obviously both wearing tuxedo pants.

RABBI: What am I, a blind man? I see London. I see France. I can see your underpants!

WALTER: Rabbi ... are you feeling all right?

RABBI: Tip top, let me tell you.

WALTER: You haven't been drinking again, have you?

(WENDY discovers a pair of scissors on the desk.)

RABBI: Just a little Manischevitz. But then I had some stuffed mushrooms. Very tasty. With a hint of nutmeg.

(WENDY motions to CLAUDIA with the scissors.)

WALTER: Oh, no! They didn't have a hint of nutmeg, did they?

RABBI: Yes. They had a *hint* of nutmeg.

WALTER: Oh, no. Mushrooms with a hint of nutmeg.

RABBI: This is bad?

WALTER: Well, sometimes they say mushrooms with a hint of ...

MITCH: Nutmeg.

WALTER: Nutmeg ... could be poisonous.

RABBI: Is that what they say?

(WENDY and CLAUDIA turn their backs and start hacking away at their attached pants with the scissors.)

WALTER: Yeah, and if they are the poisonous kind, you could be hallucinating ...

RABBI: Hallucinating?

WALTER: It's okay. Nothing to be worried about. Just

as long as you didn't mix it with wine.

RABBI: Oy God, I did. I mixed it with wine.

MITCH: Whew. Wine and poisonous mushrooms. Bad combination.

WALTER: You haven't seem any pink elephants, have you? Or invisible snakes? Or pantless men leaping?

RABBI: Oy God, I did. The last one. I saw the pantless men leaping ...

WALTER: Omigod, everybody. Keep him away from the windows.

RABBI: Why?

WALTER: You could go crazy and jump out.

RABBI: Don't let me jump out!

NOEL: *(off)* Right this way, Miss Berman.

(SFX: People in hall, flashbulbs going off.)

NOEL: *(off)* Get back! Get back, you peons. A star is coming through.

WALTER: Then you better go lie down quick, Rabbi.

MITCH: Real quick.

RABBI: Not by the windows.

WENDY: Of course not.

CLAUDIA: Come with us, Rabbi. Before it's too late.

(CLAUDIA motions that the pants are no good. WALTER and MITCH misunderstand and get the idea to put them on as the girls run with the RABBI for the adjoining room. WENDY returns for the liquor bottle and exits.)

WALTER: Thank God, we have pants.

MITCH: Let's get them on and get out of here.

(The two men leap into the pants, and discover that they are held together only by the waistband. They are crotch-less like chaps and shredded like a hula skirt.)

WALTER: I think you stretched mine.
MITCH: Are they supposed to fit like this?

(The men freeze as the door to their room opens half way. Their shredded pants fall to the floor.)

NOEL: *(calling back into the hallway)* People, please. Please clear the door so I can get Miss Berman in her room! God, it's like you never saw a superstar before! *(panicked, WALTER dives into the closet, MITCH pulls him out, WALTER pulls him out. As MITCH reaches for WALTER again, WALTER closes the door on MITCH's hand. MITCH panicked, dives under the bed as the door opens. He drags the shredded pants with him. NOEL enters to make sure the coast is clear) (to himself)* Thank Heaven for small favors. They're gone. *(turning to hallway, relieved)* Here's your room, Miss Berman.

(LAINIE BERMAN enters. She is very loud, very Vegas, and very temperamental.)

LAINIE: What the hell am I doing here?

(MR. & MRS. KIRSCHENBAUM enter after her.)

MR. KIRSCHENBAUM: Welcome to New York, Miss Berman. I am Harry Kirschenbaum, father of the bride.

LAINIE: Hey, Harry. Nice hair.

MRS. KIRSCHENBAUM: And in case you're wondering, I'm Edie Kirschenbaum, the mother of the bride.

MR. KIRSCHENBAUM: She's not wondering, Edie. Does she look like she's wondering? Now, if you don't mind, I'm talking here. *(sweetly to LAINIE)* Sorry about that, Lainie. Celebrities bring out the bumpkin in her.

LAINIE: Don't worry about it, Eddie.

MRS. KIRSCHENBAUM: That's Edie.

MR. KIRSCHENBAUM: Whatever. *(to LAINIE)* I still can't believe it. When you performed at our upholstered furniture convention in Vegas, I never would have guessed six months later, you'd be here singing at my daughter's wedding. It's like a dream.

MRS. KIRSCHENBAUM: It's like a dream.

MR. KIRSCHENBAUM: She already knows it's like a dream, Edie. I just told her it was like a dream! Now stop fawning over her like a goddam groupie. And hang up her suitbag.

MRS. KIRSCHENBAUM: Oh, yes, Miss Berman. It would make me the happiest woman alive to hang up your suitbag.

LAINIE: Thanks, Eddie.

MRS. KIRSCHENBAUM: That's Edie.

MR. KIRSCHENBAUM: *(shooting his wife a look)* Eddie's okay, too.

(EDIE hangs up LAINIE's suitbag. WALTER – hiding in the closet – happens to be leaning, arm extended, with his

back to the audience. EDIE hangs up the suitbag on his arm and closes the door.)

LAINIE: Oh, it's good to be back in New York. I like this town. It has good energy. Ooh, I can feel it pulsing through my body. *(she starts doing sexy stretching motions)* This city really gets me going, you know what I mean? *(MR. KIRSCHENBAUM chokes and does tongue-tied business behind her back)* Anyway, good to see you again, Harry.

MR. KIRSCHENBAUM: "Harry." See that, everyone? She still remembers the little people. That's why she's the star she is.

NOEL: Oh, look at the time. Oh, well. No rush. Relax, settle in, freshen up, unwind. You go on in forty-five minutes. Jesus God. It's okay. Don't rush. I'll just set your clothes out – to save you a few seconds here and there. Unless of course, you were going to wear what you have on.

LAINIE: I have a dress in my suitbag.

NOEL: *(sotto, to MRS. KIRSCHENBAUM)* Thank God. Would you be caught dead in that outfit?

(NOEL reaches in the closet and takes the suitbag which WALTER is hiding behind. NOEL carries the suitbag and WALTER – unseen by the others – to the bed, as MR. KIRSCHENBAUM closes the door behind NOEL. NOEL lies the suitbag – with WALTER under it – on the bed. MR. KIRSCHENBAUM turns back to LAINIE just as WALTER is covered up.)

MR. KIRSCHENBAUM: Don't mind Noel. He's a little nervous. Because he knows if this wedding isn't flawless I'll break off both his arms and shove them up his ass.

    NOEL: If I had a nickel for every time I heard that.

(Behind everyone's backs, MITCH reaches up and punches WALTER in the stomach. WALTER quickly gets up and crosses back, suitbag and all, to the closet without anyone seeing him. He hangs himself back up.)

    MRS. KIRSCHENBAUM: Where are the rest of your things?

    LAINIE: On their way up, Peetie.

    MRS. KIRSCHENBAUM: That's Edie.

    MR. KIRSCHENBAUM: You knew who she meant.

(NOEL notices the suitbag is gone.)

    NOEL: Didn't I just lay out your evening wear?

    LAINIE: Huh? Oh. I don't think so.

    NOEL: Yes, I did. I mean ... I could've sworn I did.

    MR. KIRSCHENBAUM: Well, you didn't. So do it now. You moron.

    NOEL: Yes sir.

(NOEL bewildered, carries the suitbag and WALTER to the bed, lays it down. MR. KIRSCHENBAUM closes the door behind him again. As WALTER is laid down, suitbag over him, MR. KIRSCHENBAUM turns back to LAINIE.)

    MRS. KIRSCHENBAUM: How was your flight in from Las Vegas, Miss Berman?

    LAINIE: Fine. If you don't mind hearing one of the

engines blow out at 30,000 feet ... *(MITCH reaches up and punches him again. WALTER walks himself back to the closet)* ... and having to emergency land in Cleveland in the middle of a hideous thunderstorm with everyone on the plane either screaming their brains out or puking their lunch up.

MRS. KIRSCHENBAUM: Pretty City, Cleveland.

MR. KIRSCHENBAUM: Noel, I told you to get her suitbag. What are you, deaf?

NOEL: *(confused)* What?

MR. KIRSCHENBAUM: Suitbag. *(yelling into NOEL's headset microphone)* Suitbag! Suitbag! Get the suitbag, idiot!

NOEL: I just ...

MR. KIRSCHENBAUM: You just what?

NOEL: I just ... was going to get it.

(He crosses for suitbag one last time. WALTER and the suitbag are moved to the bed.)

MRS. KIRSCHENBAUM: So do you get to our fair city very often, Miss Berman?

LAINIE: Manhattan? I thought you guys lived in Long Island.

(MITCH reaches up and punches the suitbag again. WALTER rises, kicks the crap out of MITCH under the bed, then walks back to the closet unnoticed.)

MRS. KIRSCHENBAUM: I ... oh ... it was just a figure of speech. Actually, if you take the train ...

MR. KIRSCHENBAUM: Hey, do us all a favor, Edie. *Take* the train.

(VINNIE enters from the front door. With a suitcase. He's a mob guy from Vegas. Very jealous. Very cafone. He sets down two bags.)

VINNIE: Could you walk ahead of me any farther? Good thing I heard your big fat mouth or I never would have found the room.

LAINIE: Ah, screw you, you big meat necked thug.

NOEL: How dare you speak to Miss Berman like this. Who is this animal?

LAINIE: My boyfriend.

NOEL: Oh ... nice to meet you, sir. Shall I pick the lint off your jacket?

(NOEL starts picking lint off VINNIE's jacket.)

VINNIE: No. Get away from me.

MR. KIRSCHENBAUM: Shut up, Noel. *(to NOEL, RE: LAINIE, sotto)* I'm only paying for the one airfare, and the one entree. Got it?

NOEL: Yes, Mr. Kirschenbaum.

LAINIE: Vinnie, where's my makeup kit?

VINNIE: How do I know? Who am I, Max Factor? You sure you don't have it?

LAINIE: Do I look like I have it?

VINNIE: Check the closet.

LAINIE: You check the closet.

(VINNIE opens the left-side closet door. The right-side closet door slides shut behind it. VINNIE turns to the open space where the right-side door was to see the door he

originally opened sliding closed as well.)

NOEL: Miss Berman, may I just say that I've been working on this wedding for over two years and you, Miss Berman, are the icing on the greatest cake I will ever bake.

LAINIE: Who the hell are you, again? The chef?

NOEL: No. I'm Noel the wedding coordinator. *(VINNIE tries the closet door again. He opens the down-stage door again. The other door slides closed in its place. He turns around to reach for the other door and sees it close behind him again, as well)* I created this wedding from nothing. You think *these* people had any taste.

LAINIE: Look who's talking about taste. You were running around the lobby with two pair of pants hanging off your back.

VINNIE: Maybe it was supposed to be a cape.

NOEL: It wasn't a cape. That was a mean cruel joke and I don't know how they got there. I'll bet it was that condescending concierge. French bastard.

(VINNIE tries the door the third time. Same business.)

VINNIE: What the hell's with this closet door?

LAINIE: How do I know? What am I, Bob Vila? I'm a singer, not a carpenter.

MR. KIRSCHENBAUM: Boy, are you. We can't wait to hear you sing.

MRS. KIRSCHENBAUM: Oh, yes. We can't wait to hear you sing. Especially: *(sings)*
EMOTIONS.
COVER ME LIKE LOTIONS ...

MR. KIRSCHENBAUM: Cover you with dirt!

VINNIE: Hey. Maybe I didn't make myself clear. Something funny is going on here!

LAINIE: Yeah, right. I got a man in the closet, you big ape. Come on out, lover! Come out so my boyfriend can shoot a few rounds into the skull of your head. *(to others)* He's so jealous. He's always checking up on me. It's suffocating. But he's Italian. What can I do.

MR. KIRSCHENBAUM: Hey, if I had a woman like your I'd be jealous, too, Vinnie. But ...

(He motions to MRS. KIRSCHENBAUM who is, conveniently for the joke, just bending over fixing her stockings.)

VINNIE: If I ever find anybody looking at you I'll kill them faster than you can say "No, Vinnie. That's just my brother."

(WALTER peeks out in horror, then closes the door.)

LAINIE: Tell you what, Vinnie. You find a strange man in this room, you got my permission. Blow his head off.

VINNIE: Hey, don't think I won't. Remember what I did to that guy in Tahoe.

LAINIE: Do I? I never ate eggplant parmigiana again.

(WALTER peeks out in disgust. He closes the door.)

VINNIE: Anyway, I can't find your stinking makeup kit. You must have left it in the lobby when you flirted with that guy in the suit.

LAINIE: The guy in the suit was the hotel manager. He was checking me in.

VINNIE: He was checking you out.

NOEL: Shall we call down for your kit?

LAINIE: No. I want Vinnie to go down and get it for me.

VINNIE: I'm not going down there.

LAINIE: Please, Vinnie. Would you please? I hate having strangers handle my luggage.

NOEL: I'm with you. I don't want people handling my hidden treasures. I mean ... *(off MR. KIRSCHENBAUM's look)* I'll be quiet now.

VINNIE: Shut up.

MR. KIRSCHENBAUM: Go with Vinnie, Noel.

VINNIE: The name's Pazooti.

NOEL: Okay, let's go, Pazooti.

(NOEL follows after him. VINNIE stops him casually by choking him.)

VINNIE: Vinnie Pazooti. That's Mr. Pazooti to you ... Liza.

(NOEL relishes the thought.)

MRS. KIRSCHENBAUM: "Pazooti?" Wasn't that the name of the mobster who blew out the brains of his uncle at the little clam house in Manhattan?

(LAINIE shoots her a look that says "Don't go there.")

VINNIE: That was another guy.

MRS. KIRSCHENBAUM: Of course it was. I could go for a little clam myself right now.

MR. KIRSCHENBAUM: How about clam *up*?

NOEL: After you, Mr. Pazooti.

LAINIE: Take your key, baby, I'll be in the shower when you get back.

VINNIE: Just remember, when you get out put on a robe. No walking around naked. Remember what I had to do to that window washer in Reno.

LAINIE: Do I? I never ate tongue again.

(WALTER reacts with horror, as VINNIE and NOEL exit. WENDY and CLAUDIA enter from the adjoining room with one pair of tuxedo pants behind CLAUDIA's backs – the RABBI's pants.)

WENDY: Hi. Daddy. Mom. *(hiccups)* Have you seen Mitch?

(MITCH peeks out and waves.)

CLAUDIA: Or Walter?

(WALTER peeks out and waves.)

MR. KIRSCHENBAUM: Why would we see them? Don't you see me talking to Lainie Berman? Wendy, Claudia, meet Lainie Berman.

LAINIE: Hi. Aren't you a pretty little bride?

WENDY: Yes. Yes I am.

(WENDY hiccups.)

LAINIE: *(to CLAUDIA)* Are you married, too?
CLAUDIA: No.
MR. KIRSCHENBAUM: It's not like we're not trying.
$12,000 for the nose job alone.

(The RABBI bursts in from the adjoining room without any pants on.)

RABBI: Hey! Look at me, everybody. Now it looks like *I* have no pants on!
MR. KIRSCHENBAUM: What the hell ...
MRS. KIRSCHENBAUM: He's drunk as a skunk.
WENDY: I am not!

(She falls on her face.)

MR. KIRSCHENBAUM: Edie, pick up your daughter. *(to LAINIE)* Forgive her. She's just like her mother. *(to RABBI)* Where are your pants?
RABBI: He's asking me? How do I know? I'm higher than a kite! Woo-boy! Like Lucy in the Sky with all those diamonds! I must be on a magic carpet ride.
LAINIE: Who is this man?
RABBI: *(crossing over)* Ooh, boy. What a hallucination this one is. I'm seeing Lainie Berman now. *(sings)*
EMOTIONS.
COVER ME LIKE LOTIONS ...
Oh, boy. It's a sexual delight this fantasy. I'm tripping, man. I'm smoking my brain!

LAINIE: Get away from me! Who is this freaking pervert?

MRS. KIRSCHENBAUM: Rabbi, I told you to sober up and get something to eat!

RABBI: I did. I ate the mushrooms!

MRS. KIRSCHENBAUM: Omigod, Harry. You don't think something's wrong with the mushrooms, do you?

MR. KIRSCHENBAUM: What, like botulism? Act casual. *MR. & MRS. KIRSCHENBAUM and the RABBI act casual)* Say nothing. *(They all say nothing. MR. KIRSCHENBAUM turns back to LAINIE with a fake smile)* Pardon me, Lainie, I mean, Miss Berman. We're just going to help Rabbi Huchelman find his pants.

MRS. KIRSCHENBAUM: Give us a hand, girls.

(WALTER reaches out for the pants CLAUDIA has. No one sees him, except for the RABBI.)

WENDY: But I'm the bride. I don't have to help anybody.

RABBI: The suitbag is moving.

LAINIE: What?

RABBI: The suitbag is moving.

(WALTER ducks back in the closet in the nick of time. Everyone turns to see the suitbag hanging still in the closet.)

MR. KIRSCHENBAUM: Oh, for Christ's Sake. That's right. The suitbag is moving. Come on, girls. Help me put him in the shower.

CLAUDIA: But ...

RABBI: The shower? What do I look like – a piece of Safeguard?

MR. KIRSCHENBAUM: *(as his wife)* "Let's use Rabbi Huchelman. My brother recommends him."

RABBI: Keep me away from the windows.

(MR. KIRSCHENBAUM, MRS. KIRSCHENBAUM exit with the RABBI, CLAUDIA and WENDY.)

LAINIE: Yeah, well.

(LAINIE takes the suitbag from WALTER and exits to the bathroom. Once gone, WALTER and MITCH pop out of their hiding spots.)

WALTER: *(sotto)* Psst. Mitch? Let's get out of here.

(SFX: Shower starting.)

MITCH: *(sotto)* How? You want to tell me how? We're in our underwear. We're trapped, I tell you. Trapped.

WALTER: *(sotto)* Lainie and Vinnie have suitcases, don't they? All we have to do is open them up, borrow some of their clothes, and get out of here. Let's go.

(They open up a suitcase. It's filled with women's clothes.)

MITCH: This feels so wrong.

WALTER: Where's Vinnie's bag? These are all Lainie Berman's clothes.

MITCH: *(holding up bra)* Look at the size of this thing.

WALTER: Would you put that back. We don't have time to fool around. The wedding's in twenty minutes!

MITCH: *(puts on a bra and wig)* Hey. Get a load of me. I'm Lainie Berman.

WALTER: *(smacking him)* Give me that. Idiot.

(Shower turns off.)

(The men freeze.)

WALTER: She's out of the shower. Quick. The adjoining room. *(They leave the open bags and run for the adjoining room – WALTER still in boxers, MITCH in the LAINIE BERMAN wig and bra, carrying a dress)* No. Wait. The Kirschenbaums are in there.

MITCH: Oh. Right. Back to the closet.

(As they duck into the closet, with the open suitcase. The adjoining door opens. WENDY and CLAUDIA enter.)

WENDY: Mitch? Psst? I brought you Rabbi Huchelman's pants.

(As WENDY looks under the bed, CLAUDIA steals the pants.)

CLAUDIA: They're Walter's pants.

WENDY: *(grabbing them back)* Mitch's.

CLAUDIA: *(grabbing them back)* Walter's ...

WENDY: *(grabbing them back)* Mitch's ... *(they start to tug of war. WENDY falls and the pants split in half)* Ooh.

Look what you did to Walter's pants!

(Knock at the door.)

    CLAUDIA: Somebody's coming. Get up!

(CLAUDIA grabs WENDY and the ripped pants and runs to the closet. WALTER opens it back up to say:)

    WALTER: Sorry. This space is taken.

(The closet door closes.)

    WENDY: I think I'm going to be sick.
    CLAUDIA: The balcony. You can get some fresh air.
    WENDY: I don't need fresh air. I need a bucket ... *(The girls exit to the balcony.) (off)* Look out, Claudia.
    CLAUDIA: *(off)* Ahhh! Wendy!!! It's all over me!

(LAINIE returns in a sexy slip and bathrobe. She feels chilly and closes the balcony door. Closes the drapes. Then goes to the front door.)

    LAINIE: Who's there?
    MR. KIRSCHENBAUM: *(off)* Mr. Kirschenbaum. *(she sighs, checks her watch. Lets him in)* Did your boyfriend find your makeup kit?
    LAINIE: Not yet. He's still down in the lobby.
    MR. KIRSCHENBAUM: Are we alone?
    LAINIE: Yes.
    MR. KIRSCHENBAUM: Then what are we waiting for? Kiss me.

(He goes to kiss her, she stops his face with her hand.)

    LAINIE: Wait. Where's your wife?
    MR. KIRSCHENBAUM: *(adjusting his broken jaw)* I sent her downstairs to check on the mushrooms.
    LAINIE: Good thinking.
    MR. KIRSCHENBAUM: Kiss me.

(He dives at her over the bed. She moves away. He falls face first onto the floor. His toupee flips up, stuck to the front of his head with toupee tape.)

    LAINIE: Wait. Where does she think you are?
    MR. KIRSCHENBAUM: Sobering up the Rabbi.
    LAINIE: Good plan.
    MR. KIRSCHENBAUM: Kiss me.

(He runs to her. She motions "wait" with her hand, and mashes him in the crotch by accident.)

    LAINIE: Wait. This isn't a good time. Vinnie will be back any second.
    MR. KIRSCHENBAUM: *(high-pitched)* I ... *(clears throat)* I ... I can't help it. You drive me crazy.
    LAINIE: I know.
    MR. KIRSCHENBAUM: Does he suspect anything?
    LAINIE: No. He's completely in the dark. Nobody knows about us. Nobody.

(WALTER and MITCH peek out, then close the door.)

MR. KIRSCHENBAUM: I'll never forget that night I met you in Vegas. I walked into the lounge, and there before me was the most beautiful woman I'd ever seen. And right behind her was you, standing on the stage, looking into my eyes like you were singing to me and me alone. That song still haunts my dreams. *(he sings)*
EMOTIONS.
COVER ME LIKE LOTIONS.
SINCE YOU LEFT ME I CRY OCEANS.
LOST WITHOUT YOUR LOVE.
    LAINIE: *(sings)*
EMOTIONS.

(WALTER and MITCH peek out, with looks of horror on their faces, holding their noses, etc. They close the closet door behind them, as WALTER casually grabs an orange from the fruit basket.)

    MR. KIRSCHENBAUM & LAINIE: *(sings)*
DRIPPING OFF LIKE LOTIONS.
    LAINIE: *(sings)*
EMOTIONS.
    MR. KIRSCHENBAUM & LAINIE: *(sings)*
CRYING TEARFUL OCEANS.
    LAINIE: *(sings)*
EMOTIONS.
    MR. KIRSCHENBAUM & LAINIE: *(sings)*
FILLED WITH DEEP DEVOTION.
    LAINIE: *(sings)*
EMOTIONS.
    MR. KIRSCHENBAUM: *(sings)*
LOST WITHOUT YOUR LOVE.

(spoken) Kiss me.

(He starts to, but there is a knock at the door. LAINIE stops his face with her hand.)

LAINIE: Wait!

MR. KIRSCHENBAUM: *(tongue swollen)* Whath whaang? Ahem. "What's wrong?"

VINNIE: *(off)* Open up, Lainie. I forgot my key!

LAINIE: All right. Quit yelling. *(to HARRY)* Quick. Hide. He'll kill you.

MR. KIRSCHENBAUM: Nyahhh. Where should I hide?

LAINIE: The closet!

(MR. KIRSCHENBAUM runs for the closet. Before he even gets to it the door opens like an elevator. He enters the closet confused. The door closes behind him, just as he starts to look for an elevator button. LAINIE opens the door to let in VINNIE.)

VINNIE: What's going on in here? I thought I heard singing.

LAINIE: Of course you heard singing. I'm a singer. I'm warming up, numbnuts. God, are you thick.

VINNIE: I didn't hear you complaining last night. You sure that was you? Sounded like a man to me.

LAINIE: I can't help it. I'm an alto. I have a very low range.

VINNIE: Since when?

LAINIE: Since forever.

VINNIE: Oh, is that right? Then sing something in your

low range, Miss Forever.

    LAINIE: Okay. Here goes. *(sings a descending low scale)*
LA, LA ...

(She lip-syncs to the basso in the closet behind her.)

    MR. KIRSCHENBAUM: *(off) (finishing the scale)*
LA, LA, LA ...

    VINNIE: That was you? Okay. So I was wrong. Sorry. Sing something else.

    LAINIE: "Sing something else?"

(MR. KIRSCHENBAUM keeps on singing. She is forced to lip sync.)

    MR. KIRSCHENBAUM: *(off) (sings)*
MAMA'S LITTLE BABY LOVES
    SHORTENIN', SHORTENIN'.
MAMA'S LITTLE BABY LOVES
    SHORTENIN' BREAD.
MAMA'S LITTLE BABY LOVES
    SHORTENIN', SHORTENIN'.
MAMA'S LITTLE BABY LOVES
    SHORTENIN' BREAD.

(LAINIE relaxes thinking it's over, then:)

PUT ON THE SKILLET.
PUT ON THE SPREAD!
MAMA'S GONNA MAKE A LITTLE
    SHORTENIN' BREAD.

(As LAINIE gets more animated with dancing arm movements.)

THAT AIN'T ALL.
SHE GONNA DO.
MAMMY'S GONNA MAKE A LITTLE
    CORNBREAD ...

(As someone shuts him up.) Ooh!

(VINNIE reacts.)

LAINIE: Ooh. Cramps. I'm not singing anymore. Now, quit smothering me and get dressed for the wedding.
VINNIE: Okay. Okay. Where's my suit, in the closet?

(Without looking in, VINNIE reaches and slides open the closet door. We see WALTER in his boxers, MITCH in a dress and wig, and MR. KIRSCHENBAUM in his tuxedo. All are frozen with fear.)

LAINIE: Omigod, Vinnie, No!

(VINNIE stops, the door closes behind him.)

VINNIE: What's wrong?
LAINIE: I forgot to pack your tuxedo.
VINNIE: What are you talking about? You never pack for me.
LAINIE: Uh ... I meant you forgot to pack your tuxedo.
VINNIE: I did not. Why are you acting so weird?

(opening door) Is something going on around here?

*(VINNIE opens the closet door again without looking to
reveal MITCH now in the long pants, WALTER in the
dress and wig and MR. KIRSCHENBAUM in the boxers.
The door closes behind VINNIE.)*

LAINIE: No.

VINNIE: Cause if I find out something's going on, you
know what'll happen. Remember that time I thought my
uncle was looking at you? And what I did to him?

LAINIE: Yes, but I told you a million times, your uncle
wasn't looking at me. He had glaucoma. He looked at
everybody like that.

VINNIE: Okay. So I was wrong that one time, but still ...
Something's weird around here.

*(He opens the closet door again to reveal MR.
KIRSCHENBAUM in the dress and wig on, MITCH in
the boxers, and WALTER in the tuxedo. All are frozen.
The door closes behind VINNIE.)*

LAINIE: How ... do you know?

VINNIE: Cause I know you like a book.

LAINIE: That would be impressive if you ever read a
book. Now, you gonna get dressed or you gonna stand there
with your thumb up your ass?

VINNIE: Those are my only two choices? Where's the
suitbag, anyway?

(He opens the closet door again to reveal an empty closet. He

opens the other side and we see MR. KIRSCHENBAUM in his tuxedo with the wig on, MITCH in the dress with the tuxedo and bra over it, and WALTER in boxers with a gray toupee on running to the other side out of VINNIE's sight.)

LAINIE: In the bathroom! *(the closet doors close)* Where do you think it is?

VINNIE: I still don't know why you took this job anyway. You don't normally sing at weddings.

LAINIE: No reason. I wanted to see the Big Apple. Is that a crime? *(someone in the closet sneezes)* Gesundheit.

VINNIE: Thank you. No. I just thought that since you never. Wait a minute. I didn't sneeze.

LAINIE: Oh. Then I guess I did.

VINNIE: The hell you did. Either I'm an idiot or somebody's in this closet.

LAINIE: *(muttered)* Two out of two.

VINNIE: Get out here! *(he tries opening the door. It won't budge)* Who's in there?

LAINIE: Nobody.

VINNIE: Who is in there?

MITCH: *(off)* Nobody.

LAINIE: See? I mean ...

(VINNIE pulls out a gun.)

VINNIE: That's it. *(VINNIE shoots the gun in the air)* Anybody who can hear my voice! You better get your ass out here on the count of three or I'm gonna blow your brains all over the wall! Got it?! One. Two. Three! *(on "three" everyone enters at once with their hands up! From the closet – WALTER in his boxers, MR. KIRSCHENBAUM in his tuxedo – toupee in his hand like a shield – with MITCH in his dress and wig clinging to him for protection. From the open balcony, a very drunk WENDY unconscious in the arms of CLAUDIA who's in her slip. And from the adjoining room, RABBI HUCKELMAN in his boxers with a towel on his head like a turban with MRS. KIRSCHENBAUM. And NOEL entering from the hallway door)* Holy shit ...

(He shoots himself in the foot, and NOEL faints as we:)

THE CURTAIN FALLS

ACT II

(Curtain rises on everyone frozen in the same positions, frozen in fear or mouths agape as VINNIE holds his gun on them.)

RABBI: You ain't gonna believe what I'm seeing now.

MRS. KIRSCHENBAUM: What is going on in here?

WALTER: Nothing. Go away.

LAINIE: Who the hell are you?

WALTER: Walter. Nice to meet you. I'm a big fan.

LAINIE: Get off of me. I've never seen this man before in my life.

VINNIE: Don't give me that.

LAINIE: I swear.

NOEL: I've got organ music starting downstairs, people.

MRS. KIRSCHENBAUM: Yes, we have organ music starting downstairs.

MR. KIRSCHENBAUM: Thanks, Edie. We didn't hear it the first nine times.

LAINIE: Who are you people? And what are you doing in here?

WALTER: Oh, not much.

LAINIE: *(to MITCH)* Why are you wearing my clothes?

MITCH: Oh, are these yours? I'm sorry. I had no idea.

NOEL: Good color on you.

MITCH: Thank you ... I mean ...

MR. KIRSCHENBAUM: What *are* you people all doing

61

in here?

CLAUDIA: Oh, we're just looking at the view.

MR. KIRSCHENBAUM: Where is *your* dress?!

CLAUDIA: On the balcony.

MITCH: *(re: LAINIE)* This is hers.

MR. KIRSCHENBAUM: Not you!

CLAUDIA: Wendy threw up on it.

LAINIE: You threw up on my dress?

CLAUDIA: My dress!

VINNIE: What was she doing with your dress?

MRS. KIRSCHENBAUM: How could you, Wendy?

WENDY: Like this. Bleech.

NOEL: The wedding starts in fifteen minutes!

CLAUDIA: I cleaned it, Noel.

MR. KIRSCHENBAUM: How long have you all been in here?

WALTER: *(sings)*
EMOTIONS.
COVER ME LIKE LOTIONS.
LOST WITHOUT YOUR LOVE.

(LAINIE and MR. KIRSCHENBAUM react.)

VINNIE: That's Lainie's song! That's it. Everybody. Hands up.

(They all raise their hands.)

RABBI: Look how high they go.

(CLAUDIA raises her hands and drops WENDY on her butt.)

WENDY: I'm awake! I ... huh?

LAINIE: What are you gonna do, big man? Kill us all?

VINNIE: *(aiming at WALTER)* Maybe I will. And he's first.

WALTER: No wait. You got the wrong guy.

VINNIE: You sang the song.

WALTER: He sang the song first!

MR. KIRSCHENBAUM: He's a liar. I can't even sing.

MITCH: I'll say.

RABBI: I can sing like a bird. *(sings)*
EMOTIONS.
SOMETHING – SOMETHING.
LAND O'GOSHENS ...

NOEL: I don't have time for this. *(VINNIE shoots his gun over NOEL's head) (posing nonchalantly)* Oh, look at the time.

VINNIE: Shut up. *(to WALTER)* You picked the wrong guy to make a fool out of, you.

WALTER: I'm sorry. Tell me who the right guy is and I'll make a fool out of *him.* I mean ...

LAINIE: Vinnie, you big stupid jerk. You kill him and there'll be eight witnesses.

VINNIE: You're right. I guess I'll have to kill you all. *(everyone freaks out)* Okay, everybody. Line up. I think I can do this in one shot.

(They do.)

MRS. KIRSCHENBAUM: Omigod ...

WENDY: Thanks a lot, Lainie Berman.

WALTER: I told you we should have eloped.

MITCH: And to think I never got to see the Ice Capades.

MR. KIRSCHENBAUM: Shut up, you.

CLAUDIA: I knew I'd die single.

MR. KIRSCHENBAUM: So did I.

RABBI: Is it just me or does anyone else see that hooded man with the big sickle?

VINNIE: You all die on the count of three.

MRS. KIRSCHENBAUM: Oh, God ...

WENDY: I would be wearing white for this.

VINNIE: One!

MITCH: I think my sphincter just relaxed.

VINNIE: Two!

RABBI: Lucky bastard.

VINNIE: Thr...

WALTER: *(as VINNIE aims his gun)* Wait! This is insane. *(crossing to VINNIE)* I'm not fooling around with Lainie, Mr. Pazooti. You have to believe me.

LAINIE: He's right, Vinnie. He's not even my type. Look at him. That nose. Those legs. And what's with the hair?

VINNIE: Yeah. What is with that hair?

(LAINIE and VINNIE laugh. The others join in. WALTER is humiliated.)

WALTER: All right. All right.

MITCH: And look at his ears.

MRS. KIRSCHENBAUM: Yes, Mr. Pazooti. There's clearly been a misunderstanding here. That young man is marrying my daughter Wendy.

(VINNIE lowers his gun. Everyone drops their hands, relaxed.)

CLAUDIA: No, he's not, Mom.

(VINNIE aims his gun. All the hands go back up.)

WALTER: *(desperate)* Yes, he is, Mom!

(VINNIE lowers his gun. All the hands relax.)

CLAUDIA: No, he's not.

(VINNIE raises his gun. All the hands go up.)

WENDY: Actually, we're not sure.

(VINNIE doesn't know where to put the gun – up or down. The hands of the others follow the gun and go up, down and sideways, etc.)

MR. KIRSCHENBAUM: "Not sure?" This thing's costing me $100,000!

WALTER: *(eyeing gun, winking)* Sure we're sure, "darling."

CLAUDIA: "Darling?"

MRS. KIRSCHENBAUM: Claudia. Shut up. The man has a gun. A pistol. A piece.

VINNIE: Which is it?

WALTER: Take your pick. They all mean the same thing.

(VINNIE forces WALTER to his knees.)

    WENDY: Daddy, say something.
    WALTER: *(to MR. KIRSCHENBAUM)* Don't let him do this, sir.
    MRS. KIRSCHENBAUM: He's going to kill him, Harry. Say something.

(All eyes are on HARRY.)

    MR. KIRSCHENBAUM: How could you, Walter?

(He winks to LAINIE that everything's okay.)

    LAINIE: What?
    WALTER: I'm not ...
    MR. KIRSCHENBAUM: *(sotto to LAINIE)* Go with me on this, Lainie.
    LAINIE: Harry!
    MR. KIRSCHENBAUM: What kind of a sick bastard cheats on my daughter? I could kill you myself. Here, Vinnie. Give me the gun!
    VINNIE: Get back, rug head.
    MR. KIRSCHENBAUM: *(adjusting toupee in paranoia)* Who told him?
    CLAUDIA: You know about us, Daddy?
    MR. KIRSCHENBAUM: Know about what?
    CLAUDIA: About me and Walter?
    MRS. KIRSCHENBAUM: *You* and Walter?
    VINNIE: You and Lainie *and* Walter?
    WALTER: No. No Lainie.

VINNIE: Who's Walter?

LAINIE: Aren't you Walter?

WALTER: It depends who he's going to shoot.

MR. KIRSCHENBAUM: Wait a minute. You and Walter? I'm talking about Wendy.

WENDY: And Mitch?

MRS. KIRSCHENBAUM: Mitch?

WENDY: Who told you about Mitch?

VINNIE: Who's Mitch?

MR. KIRSCHENBAUM: What the hell's going on with Wendy and Mitch?

VINNIE: What happened to Walter?

WENDY: I was cheating with Mitch!

MR. KIRSCHENBAUM: You were what?

MRS. KIRSCHENBAUM: Harry!

WALTER: Wendy!

CLAUDIA: Walter!

MR. KIRSCHENBAUM: Mitch?!

VINNIE: Lainie ...

*(Everyone freaks out. Except for NOEL, who has had enough.
He pulls VINNIE's shoulder.)*

NOEL: You're doing nothing, mister. I have been working two years to make this wedding come together with the precision timing of a space shuttle launch. Two years of blood, sweat and, oh yes, many a tear. Now I don't give a fly fart who your girlfriend's sleeping with. Nothing's going to interfere with this wedding from starting in exactly five minutes and· forty-three seconds. You hear me? Nothing! *(VINNIE fires his gun over NOEL's head) (immediately crumbling)* Just kidding! Can't you take a joke!! *(to himself)* I think I just wet myself.

(He sheepishly walks away into the corner of the room.)

> WENDY: Won't anybody do anything?
> NOEL: Omigod. The wedding photographer. Gotta go.

(NOEL turns off the lights, and exits to the hallway. It is pitch black yet we can see the skyline out the balcony and the hall lights when NOEL exits. Scuffles start in the dark as everyone tries to get away. In the dark we hear:)

> WENDY: The lights!
> MRS. KIRSCHENBAUM: Somebody get the gun!
> MITCH: Get the gun!
> MR. KIRSCHENBAUM: Get the gun!
> WALTER: You get the gun!
> VINNIE: Freeze!

(Everyone does as WENDY turns on the lights. We reveal VINNIE, stage-right, has the gun to MITCH's head. We see everyone else frozen, stage-left, in running positions trying to escape out the balcony.)

> MITCH: We'll always have Paris.
> VINNIE: Which one are you again?
> MITCH: Mitch.
> VINNIE: Wrong guy! I want either Walter, Eddie or Harry.

(As WALTER and HARRY point at each other, WENDY hits the light switch. In the dark we hear another scuffle.)

MRS. KIRSCHENBAUM: Run away.

CLAUDIA: Run away!

VINNIE: Who was that? Eddie or Harry?

LAINIE: I think it was Tweetie.

MRS. KIRSCHENBAUM: That's Edie!

VINNIE: Freeze! I got you now you slimy bastard! *(everyone does as VINNIE turns on the lights. We reveal VINNIE has the gun to WENDY's head. Everyone else is running for the front door.)* Sorry. Wrong slimy bastard.

WENDY: God, you've got big hands.

RABBI: And those feet are no small potatoes either. They're like shoe boxes.

(LAINIE turns off the light. In the dark we hear another scuffle.)

CLAUDIA: Somebody stop him!

LAINIE: Hey. Get your hand off of me.

RABBI: Sorry. I thought that was the light switch.

LAINIE: Well, it's not.

RABBI: Then could I have my wrist watch back?

MR. KIRSCHENBAUM: Stand back. I've got him. I've got him! Take that. And that! And that!! *(the lights come up to reveal VINNIE at the light switch, stage-left, and MR. KIRSCHENBAUM, stage-right, pummeling WENDY in the stomach. As she leaps in the air with each punch, the others stand horrified, center-stage)* And that! And ... oh ...

(He realizes who it is and stops.)

VINNIE: Asshole. *(WENDY turns off the lights. Everyone runs around in the dark)* Go ahead. Turn the lights off. I can still *hear* you, can't I?
WALTER: Yeah. But you can't hear us with the radio on.

(In the dark, WALTER turns on the radio. A insanely quick-paced jazz piece comes on the radio. Example piece: "Yeah Man" by Count Basie. VINNIE turns on the lights. Everyone is gone. He draws his gun. And to the radio music, the following ballet takes place, in as fast a speed as humanly possible.)

(VINNIE checks out the drapes. There is no one there.)

(He checks out the bathroom. There is no one there.)

(He checks out the closet. There is no one there.)

(VINNIE stands scratching his head, down-stage, by the front door, as everyone climbs out from under the bed and runs to various places, scattering like cockroaches. The RABBI runs off to the bathroom. MR. and MRS. KIRSCHENBAUM hide behind the balcony drapes. WENDY and CLAUDIA hide inside the closet. LAINIE tries pleading with VINNIE to stop all this nonsense. The last two out from under the bed are WALTER and MITCH, one from each side. They return to hide under the bed as:)

(VINNIE turns to see LAINIE. He shoves her back onto the
    bed   as   he   runs   to   the   drapes   after   MR.
    KIRSCHENBAUM who he sees peeking out. As VINNIE
    goes behind the drapes, down-stage, MR. and MRS.
    KIRSCHENBAUM run out of the drapes up-stage and
    leap across the bed, running into the closet. VINNIE
    follows. WALTER and MITCH dodge the feet.)

(Running from their parents, WENDY and CLAUDIA are
    chased out from the closet and hide back behind the
    drapes. They motion LAINIE to join them. She does.)

(VINNIE follows through the closet – gun drawn – to see
    LAINIE and MR. and MRS. KIRSCHENBAUM join
    WENDY and CLAUDIA hiding behind the drapes.)

(VINNIE approaches the huge bulge of drapes. He sneaks up
    on them and pounces them, revealing there is no one
    behind them. He scratches his head.)

(He looks under the bed. He sees two feet sticking out. They
    are MITCH's. VINNIE pulls on them. MITCH's legs
    stretch out from stage-left as WALTER's head stretches
    out the other end. It looks like one incredibly long body.)

(He pulls three times. On the fourth try, WALTER pulls
    himself up stage-left. VINNIE drops MITCH's feet to
    chase WALTER in three clockwise circles around the
    room and over the bed.)

(As soon as he is free – and while VINNIE is chasing

WALTER – MITCH crosses to the large piece of luggage, stage-right, and opens the suitcase in an upright position in front of the desk.)

(On the third loop around the room, WALTER dives head first into the open suitcase. MITCH quickly closes it up behind him and takes the "moving" suitcase next to the bed as VINNIE stares in astonishment.) *

(MITCH sets the suitcase down next to the bed, center-stage, and WALTER crawls out of it, nonchalantly dusting himself off and exiting with MITCH to the bathroom. VINNIE takes the suitcase from MITCH, places it by the desk, opens it and scratches his head and tries the same dive into the suitcase and smashes his head on the suitcase and the desk.)

(WALTER and MITCH enter from the bathroom with sheets tied together -- tied around MITCH's waist.)

(WALTER motions for MITCH to jump off the balcony. As WALTER goes to tie the sheets to the bed, MITCH jumps seemingly to his death. The sheets slip out of WALTER's hands and follow MITCH off the side of the balcony to the street below. WALTER exits out the balcony, stage-left, exiting towards the adjoining room side of the balcony just as VINNIE starts to come around.)

(The adjoining room opens and a line of people, led by WENDY and ending with CLAUDIA, enter – on the run. WENDY followed by LAINIE, then MR.

* See page 88.

*KIRSCHENBAUM, then MRS. KIRSCHENBAUM, then a
perplexed NOEL, then CLAUDIA. They figure eight the
room, for as they see VINNIE wake up they run back off
the balcony door.)*

*(As the mad conga line figure eights the room, CLAUDIA flies
off the end. The RABBI, entering from the bathroom,
takes NOEL's extended hand and joins the line as they
pull him off the balcony exit. VINNIE sees this line of
people and chases after them off through the balcony.
CLAUDIA follows VINNIE off.)*

*(One by one they all return from the adjoining room. VINNIE
is supposedly chasing them. WENDY, the first in the
door, grabs a metal tray off the bar, getting an idea to
bash in VINNIE's head. LAINIE tries pleading with her
not to do it. WENDY is adamant. The line wraps around
into a straight line, with WENDY, stage-left and the
RABBI ending stage-right.)*

*(Sadly, VINNIE never enters, and CLAUDIA does – getting
bashed in the face with the tray. She collapses on the
floor, face down, head under the bed, as:)*

*(MR. KIRSCHENBAUM gets an idea and takes the ice bucket
and dumps a sheet of ice cubes all over the floor, starting
at the adjoining room door, stage-left and backing up all
the way to the front door, stage-right. He explains
VINNIE will trip and fall. Everyone lines up waiting.)*

(VINNIE enters – but not by the adjoining room – by the front

door. Everyone screams and tries running the opposite way.)

(Everyone tries running away – right into the ice cubes and continually trip and fall over and over again. Doing buck and wings, trenches and general silliness. VINNIE tries after them falling as well.)

(WALTER and MITCH return from the balcony covered in ripped awnings and flags. They join the "line dance" – like specialty number as everyone slips so much they involuntarily buck and wing down the center of the group one at a time at an even more intense pace.)

(After a coincidentally synchronized bit of buck and winging, everyone falls free form and bounces off the bed and floor. As VINNIE slips, the gun gets tossed up in the air – first caught by WALTER, then NOEL, then MR. KIRSCHENBAUM, then WALTER then and finally:)

(Back to VINNIE, who nonchalantly holds it on everyone as they fall spread-eagle and spent on the final note of the song. VINNIE turns off the radio.)

VINNIE: Now, what was I saying?

MR. KIRSCHENBAUM: *(re: WALTER)* I don't remember, but you were about to shoot *him*.

LAINIE: He was not!

WALTER: Thanks a lot ... Harry!

VINNIE: "Harry?" Aha!

(As VINNIE goes to shoot HARRY, MRS. KIRSCHENBAUM grabs the gun and slaps VINNIE in the face.)

MRS. KIRSCHENBAUM: Give me that. What the hell's the matter with you? You think I'm going to stand here and let you shoot my husband?

MR. KIRSCHENBAUM: Thank you, Edie.

MRS. KIRSCHENBAUM: If anybody's going to shoot him, it's going to be me!

(She aims at HARRY.)

WENDY: Mom!

WALTER: Don't talk back to your mother, Wendy.

WENDY: Don't shoot him.

MR. KIRSCHENBAUM: Thank you, Wendy.

WENDY: If he's dead, who's gonna give me away?

(NOEL raises his hand.)

MR. KIRSCHENBAUM: Take it easy, Edie. Give me the gun.

LAINIE: Yeah. Give him the gun, Beedie.

MRS. KIRSCHENBAUM: It's Edie! And the next one who screws it up gets a bullet right in the face. Now listen to me. All of you. I'm here for a wedding, and a wedding is what we're going to have. So, no false moves ... *(taking WENDY hostage at gun point)* Or the little bride gets it. Got it? *(Everyone nods.)* Now do exactly as I say. Start moving! *(MRS. KIRSCHENBAUM motions with her gun. Everybody starts "moving in place.")* No! Over there! *(she motions, stage-left and everyone but VINNIE lines up, stage-left)* Let's go. We're getting dressed. We're going downstairs. And we're getting married. *(to NOEL)* You! Get pants. Three pair. *(NOEL exits, wetting himself again) (to WENDY)* You. Get your veil on! You've got an aisle to march down.

WENDY: But Mother ... Walter and I have problems.

MRS. KIRSCHENBAUM: I don't give a shit. Nothing's interfering with this wedding. You hear me? Nothing! I'm tired! I'm angry! And I'm the mother of the bride goddammit. Don't mess with me.

(WENDY exits quickly to the adjoining room.)

VINNIE: *(grabbing his gun back)* Give me that. I got unfinished business here.

(LAINIE smacks him in the back of the head.)

LAINIE: What's the matter with you? God, are you a jerk. Don't you see this is their wedding day?

VINNIE: You and Toupee Harry over there are playing ba-da-bing ba-da-bing and I'm not supposed to get emotional?

LAINIE: I never ba-da-banged with Harry, you big fat head. I've just been leading him on to drive you crazy.

WALTER: For six months?

LAINIE: It's possible. I'm a great tease. Right, Harry?

MR. KIRSCHENBAUM: *(mesmerized)* Huh?

VINNIE: Are you telling me you never ... ?

LAINIE: Not even once. Look at him. Would you? Would anybody?

MITCH: I would. If, you know, I'd been in prison a really long time.

LAINIE: I just wanted to make you jealous.

VINNIE: What are you talking about? I'm always jealous.

LAINIE: But never enough to marry me. I mean, Jeez, Vinnie, what do I have to do? We've been going out for sixteen years. I'm starting to think we got no future.

MR. KIRSCHENBAUM: Hold on there. You were just using me to get to him?

LAINIE: Sorry, Harry. But didn't you find it weird that nothing happened between us in the entire six months?

MR. KIRSCHENBAUM: Not really.

MRS. KIRSCHENBAUM: He wouldn't find that odd.

VINNIE: We got something special here, Lainie. I'm not messing it up by marrying you.

RABBI: Young man. Take the chance. Everything in this world is so temporary. Marriage is the last time in our lives that we get a chance to make something that could last forever. Take the chance. Go for the love that will last for all eternity. *(everyone looks happy)* And if things don't work out? Divorce her! It's the 90's. Who the hell cares.

MITCH: Jeez, he must really be drunk.

RABBI: No, I sobered up. But I am stoned out of my skull.

WALTER: Rabbi. I don't know how to tell you this. You aren't stoned at all. We made all that mushroom stuff up to try and fool you.

RABBI: What mushrooms? I found some reefer in the housekeeper's cart. What a day! I am the Walrus. Coo-coo-ka-choo.

VINNIE: The Rabbi makes sense.

(He starts to kneel.)

LAINIE: What are you doing?

VINNIE: Proposing.

LAINIE: Wait. Not yet. I waited sixteen years for this. And I'm not doing it in my underwear. *(she starts off to get dressed) (to MR. KIRSCHENBAUM)* Sorry, Harry.

(She exits.)

MR. KIRSCHENBAUM: Well ... looks like you win me back, Edie.

MRS. KIRSCHENBAUM: *(grabbing gun back)* Think again, Harry. I've already wasted twenty-eight years. I'm not spending one more second with you, you pompous, rude, obnoxious sexist, blowhard pain in my big fat ass.

MR. KIRSCHENBAUM: Wait a minute. Who do you think you're talking to?

VINNIE: She's talking to you, you piece of shit.

MR. KIRSCHENBAUM: But, Edie. You can't throw me out. Where will you go? You'll be left all alone, Edie. All alone. You know nobody else is gonna want you.

RABBI: You're wrong there. I would.

MRS. KIRSCHENBAUM: Rabbi Huchelman.

RABBI: Maybe it's the ganja talking, but Edie ... You're one fine woman. You got a nice smell to your breath. Like fresh towels.

MRS. KIRSCHENBAUM: Really?

MR. KIRSCHENBAUM: Oh, brother.

(CLAUDIA crawls out from under the bed, a handkerchief held up to her smashed in face.)

CLAUDIA: *(in a nasal voice)* Oh, Walter. I feel like this is all my fault.

WALTER: Hm? Oh. I forgot you were even here.

CLAUDIA: If we hadn't ... ba-da-bing-ed, we'd be cutting the cake by now.

WALTER: Don't blame yourself for this mess, Claudia. It takes two to ... *(CLAUDIA lowers the handkerchief, showing us her big malformed hook nose)* ... What happened to your nose?

CLAUDIA: I broke it.

WALTER: No!

MR. KIRSCHENBAUM: $12,000 down the toilet.

VINNIE: You talk again ... I kill you with my bare hands.

CLAUDIA: I knew it. You don't love me for me. You only loved me for my nose.

WALTER: That's ridiculous. I would never ... Christ, Claudia. Our kids could've *looked* like that.

CLAUDIA: I can't marry you, Walter. I want a man who loves me for me.

MRS. KIRSCHENBAUM: And you'll fine one, Claudia. You're a very pretty girl.

VINNIE: She's right. Think better of yourself. If I wasn't already betrothed, I'd be giving you the business myself.

(WENDY enters.)

CLAUDIA: Thanks. I feel so much better now.

MRS. KIRSCHENBAUM: Good. Then go get dressed.

You're the first one down the aisle.
    CLAUDIA: Yes, Mom.

(She exits to the next room.)

    WALTER: Wendy?
    WENDY: Yeah?
    WALTER: Can you ever forgive me?
    WENDY: No. Can you ever forgive me?
    WALTER: Not really.
    WENDY: I'm sorry I went with Mitch. But ... I'd never
been with anyone but you and I didn't want to spend the rest
of my life wondering. And Mitch was there, and, well, we did
think you were going to die, Walter.
    WALTER: Oh, that's right. I forgot about that part.
    RABBI: And what did you learn from this experience,
Wendy?
    WENDY: I'm not sure, Rabbi. It was always over so
fast ...

(All eyes look to MITCH.)

    MITCH: I may be fast. But I'm accurate.
    WENDY: *(to WALTER)* So, do you still want to go
through with this?
    WALTER: Yes. Yes, I do. Because the truth is, the entire
time I was with her, I was thinking about you. And I don't
want to spend the rest of my life with her thinking about you.
I want to spend the rest of my life with you ... thinking about
her.
    WENDY: Oh, Walter ...

MR. KIRSCHENBAUM: Oh. She's her mother's daughter, all right.

VINNIE: I warned you three times.

(VINNIE punches MR. KIRSCHENBAUM in the stomach, flipping his toupee onto the floor.)

MR. KIRSCHENBAUM: Ooh. Right in my money clip.

(NOEL enters with three pair of pants, and two pair of shoes. WALTER, MITCH and the RABBI put them on.)

NOEL: I'm back. I'm back and I'm with pants and shoes! Everyone still alive? Perfect. Okay. We're right on time. If there's one thing I'm good at, it's pulling things off. It's time, everybody! Where's Miss Berman?

(LAINIE BERMAN enters in her dress. She looks marvelous.)

LAINIE: Here I am. How do I look?

NOEL: Like a queen! *(MR.. KIRSCHENBAUM chokes)* Now to re-cap, Miss Berman. You'll open with the "Theme to Ice Castles." Then after the trumpet fanfare you begin the "O'Promise Me – Drink to Me Only With Thine Eyes" medley. And remember, if I hear one note of that God Awful "Emotions Cover Me Like Lotions," I'll cover *you* with lotions!

MRS. KIRSCHENBAUM: Shouldn't we be getting downstairs?

NOEL: Just as soon as the photographer gets here. The photographer! Where the hell is the photographer!

(CLAUDIA enters from the adjoining room, dressed. With a drop-dead gorgeous photographer.)

PHOTOGRAPHER: Here I am.

CLAUDIA: Everyone. Meet Eddie. The bridal photographer.

VINNIE: So *that's* Eddie.

PHOTOGRAPHER: Why doesn't everybody get together for a group photo?

(Everyone gets together, center-stage, crunching in for a good shot.)

CLAUDIA: He went to the wrong room by mistake. Isn't that cute?

PHOTOGRAPHER: *(flirting)* Who knows? Maybe it was the right room.

(They flirt.)

MRS. KIRSCHENBAUM: Isn't this romantic? Everyone's finding true love.

MITCH: Noel?

NOEL: Yes?

MITCH: If you're free Friday, I have tickets to "Sunset Boulevard."

NOEL: *(sotto)* I'm at the Sheraton.

(They exchange a look.)

WENDY: And look at Daddy, everyone. He's so happy,

he's crying.

MR. KIRSCHENBAUM: Vinnie hit me really hard.

NOEL: Here we go, everybody. Let me inspect you. Chin up. Chest out. *(to LAINIE)* You. Chest in. Well, do the best you can ...

PHOTOGRAPHER: One, two and ... three.

(A flash goes off as everyone smiles for the camera.)

NOEL: And now ... it's magic time. Battle stations. Gentlemen, downstairs. Ladies, pinch your cheeks and follow me. If there's one thing Noel Carlo Schiavone knows how to do, it's get a wedding started on time. All right, everyone, let's go! Onward ho! *(he marches out the door. No one follows. They just all look uncomfortable. NOEL re-enters)* What's wrong? I said "Onward ho!" So ... onward ho! Follow me!

WALTER: We can't.

NOEL: Why not?

WALTER: Uh ...

CLAUDIA: We're stuck.

(We reveal all the dresses and tuxedo pants are hooked together.)

NOEL: Stuck? Stuck how?

WALTER: Stuck-stuck.

NOEL: Like a dog's-stuck? ...

(As everyone tugs at their clothing, they topple forward in an entwined clump of chaos. NOEL freaks out as:)

THE CURTAIN FALLS

PROPERTY LIST

2 Lamps
Telephone, Radio
Various Liquors, Including Vodka
Glasses
Ice Bucket, Ice
Leather-Bound Room Service Menu
Tray
Catch-All Bag
Electric Razor
Fruit Basket, Oranges
Two Pair of Men's Tuxedo Pants on Hanger
Katuba
Large Expensive Suitbag
Two Matching Pieces of Luggage
    (Largest One Rigged With False Back)
Woman's Clothes Packed in Suitcase, Woman's Bra,
    Woman's Glittery Cocktail Dress
Woman's Wig (To Match Lainie Berman's Hair)
Luggage Rack
Large Bridal Bouquet
Two Shredded Black Tuxedo Pants
    (Doubles for Wendy & Claudia attachable gag pants)
Bath Towel, Hand Towel, Bed Sheets

PERSONAL PROPS

(WALTER) Watch
(MRS. KIRSCHENBAUM) Purse
(NOEL) Scissors, Head Set
(LAINIE) Watch
(VINNIE) Starter's Pistol, Holster

COSTUME PLOT

WALTER:
Black tuxedo, white tuxedo shirt, lavender bow tie, lavender cummerbund, lavender boutonniere, boxer shorts, white t-shirt, black socks, black dress shoes *(tuxedo pants should have a spring clip sewn to right side of waist band near zipper to connect with ring on CLAUDIA's dress).*

WENDY:
Wedding gown with puffed sleeves, detachable full overskirt with large bow and 12 foot train *(gown should have peplum at waist to hide small strong metal ring sewn to right side of waist at front to connect with clip sewn to left side of MITCH's tuxedo pants. Overskirt should fasten with large hook and eyes for quick and easy removal. Underskirt of dress should be straight, ankle length and simple with a back slit for easy mobility.)* Shoulder length veil *(easily removable)*, white pumps, bouquet and large white satin bridal bag (to hide MITCH's tuxedo pants).

CLAUDIA:
Ankle length, lavender, taffeta bridesmaid gown with full skirt, peplum and *very* large puffed sleeves, and bows on the skirt at knee level on the sides *(the bow on the left side hides a small, strong metal ring sewn to the skirt which will connect with the pants for the opening scene. There should also be a ring sewn to the waist on the left side under the peplum for later use.)* Oversize lavender

hair bow, dyed to match shoes, lavender full slip and
small bouquet.

MITCH:
Black tuxedo, white tuxedo shirt, lavender bow tie,
lavender cummerbund, lavender boutonniere, white t-
shirt, boxer shorts, high black socks, black dress shoes
*(tuxedo pants should have a spring clip sewn to left side
of waist band near zipper to connect with ring on
WENDY's dress.)*
(Into:) Hot pink, marabou-trimmed, sleeveless babydoll
nightie worn *over* tuxedo shirt with bow tie,
cummerbund and boxers with black socks and wig styled
like LAINIE BERMAN.

LAINIE BERMAN:
Black high heeled boots, form fitting black leather pants,
lacy body suit, tight black leather jacket and black
shoulder bag.
(Into:) Black full slip, black panty-hose, black pumps
and bright red, above the knee Chinese robe.
(Into:) Stunning full-length sleeveless blue sequined
gown with low sweet heart neckline *(over same slip, hose
and pumps)*.

NOEL:
Black "rapper" pants tucked into black suede ankle
boots, white wing collar tuxedo shirt, black bolero cut
tuxedo jacket, black draw-string bolo neck tie, lavender
boutonniere and small headset.

MR. KIRSCHENBAUM:
Black tuxedo, white tuxedo shirt, black bow tie and cummerbund, black socks, black dress shoes, white t-shirt, boxers, lavender boutonniere, bad toupee attached with toupee tape, not spirit gum.

MRS. KIRSCHENBAUM:
Lavender beaded chiffon mother-of-the-bride dress, silver shoes, silver evening bag, large corsage, pearl necklace, large pearl earrings, nude stockings.

RABBI HUCHELMAN:
Poorly fitting black suit, dress shirt, tie, prayer shawl, white yarmulke, white shirt, boxer shorts, white socks, black sock garters and black dress shoes.

VINNIE:
Black Armani suit, pale pink dress shirt, black tie, pale pink pocket square, black socks, black dress shoes, black shoulder holster under jacket and large pinkie ring.

EDDIE:
Black tuxedo, white shirt, black bowtie, black socks, black dress shoes, camera with shoulder strap.

THE CLOSET BIT:

Because of the time allowed MITCH, WALTER and MR. KIRSCHENBAUM to exchange clothes during the "closet bit" towards the end of ACT I, the costumes must be rigged for quick changes with minimal help from a dresser off-stage of the closet.

MITCH's babydoll nightie should open completely at the center back and close with Velcro tabs like a hospital gown.

MR. KIRSCHENBAUM, after joining WALTER in the closet, changes into a duplicate tuxedo that has the jacket and pants joined at the waist *(like a jumpsuit)* and has been split down the center back to the inseam. It closes with Velcro tabs. He retains his tux shirt and accessories. During intermission he can change back into the "real" tuxedo.

WALTER remains in his boxers and shirt.

THE SUITCASE BIT:

Prior to WALTER diving through the suitcase, it is placed against the stage right wall. Directly behind the suitcase is a hinged piece of wall that is lifted up and secured. As WALTER dives head first through the hinged doors at the back of the suitcase, he is also diving through the set. As soon as he's through, drop the hinged set wall and secure in lower position. A second opening

in the set behind the up-stage center bed will allow him
to make his reappearance out the suitcase when MITCH
moves it to the bed. Attach neckties to the inside of the
suitcase to help cover WALTER's disappearance. And
tell him to watch his back when he dives.

MITCH APPEARING UNDER WENDY's WEDDING DRESS:

An opening in the wall underneath the headboard will
allow MITCH to crawl under the bed in time to slip under
the wedding dress when CLAUDIA walks WENDY to
the foot of the bed. WALTER cues MITCH after
WENDY is in position and can also steady the bedspread
and the wedding gown from shifting while MITCH
crawls into place. When in position, WALTER and
MITCH can tap WENDY's leg as a cue for her cross
down-stage right with the two men hidden underneath
her dress.